To Izzy.

Thanks to Jane, Richard, Chloe & Sophie.

Matador
Unit E2 Airfield Business Park,
Harrison Road, Market Harborough,
Leicestershire. LE16 7UL
Tel: 0116 2792299
Email: books@troubador.co.uk
Web: www.troubador.co.uk/matador
Twitter: @matadorbooks

ISBN 978 1803137 209

British Library Cataloguing in Publication Data.
A catalogue record for this book is available from the British Library.

Matador is an imprint of Troubador Publishing Ltd

Illustration and Design by: Happydesigner

NAUGHTY IZZY
Breaks the Rules

by **Maria King**

Illustrated by **Sarah-Leigh Wills**

Izzy the dog is jumping with glee
as Dad struggles with the Christmas tree.
He's trying to squeeze it through the door,
pine needles falling all over the floor.

Oh! This is fun, this is fun!
thinks Izzy as she jumps about
with Chloe and Sophie.

They certainly have a brilliant time,
decorating the tree, which looks so fine.
Izzy's busy; she has tinsel on her head,
and lots of baubles are in her bed.

Presents are put under the tree.
Izzy wonders what they could be.
Perhaps a stick, or a ball on a string
or something else that she could fling.

She races around, always in the way
as her family get ready to leave today.
Mum's taking the girls off to their schools,
so she calls Izzy and spells out the rules.

"Now be good, Izzy; don't lie on the chairs
or the beds, or they'll be covered in hairs,
and don't touch the presents under the tree.
Show us all how good you can be."

"I've put your biscuits by the kitchen door.
Please don't fling them all over the floor."
Mum and the girls set off on their ride.
Izzy waits and listens, head cocked on one side.

She looks at the tree, gifts all around.
What were the rules? She's there in a bound.
She sniffs and she rummages. Was that a squeak?
It's probably a new toy; she lost hers last week.

It is a toy! She throws it in the air,
into the hall and onto the stair,
then into the kitchen, what a high throw . . .
but it doesn't come down! Oh no! Oh no!

It's on the worktop; she runs around.
Has she lost it, never to be found?
She peers over the top; her eyes widen with joy.
What marvellous luck, she's forgotten her toy.

Within reach of her paws, smelling divine,
is a joint of **COLD BEEF!** Izzy thinks, All mine!
She drags the beef back to the tree,

Yummy! Yummy!

thinks naughty Izzy.

She fills her tum and gets grease everywhere,
all over the presents and stuck in her hair.
Then she takes a nap – **upstairs on Mum's bed!**
It's where she gets the sun on her head.

Uh oh! She's awake and back at the tree.
Is that DOGGY chocolate? Best sniff and see.
A doggy choccy treat dangles on her nose,
covered in tin foil, Izzy thinks, **Here goes!**

She licks and sucks all the chocolate out,
then smacks her lips and runs all about.
She jumps on the chair and onto the floor,
when suddenly! She hears keys in the door!

"This is strange," says Mum. "She's not under our feet.
Izzy's always right here to greet and meet.
Unless . . . **Oh no!** What has she done?
IZZY! IZZY! Come here right now! **COME!**"

Izzy peers round the door,
sees her mum and thinks . . .
I might have had
too much fun!

Beef in her hair, chocolate all over her face,
Mum immediately knows what's taken place.
Both the girl's giggle; Izzy's looking glum.
"Off to bed, Izzy!" says a rather cross Mum.
"If you can fit in it . . . with that very large tum!"

BUT

Izzy was thinking as she waddled away

Christmas is brilliant

I hope it's here to stay.